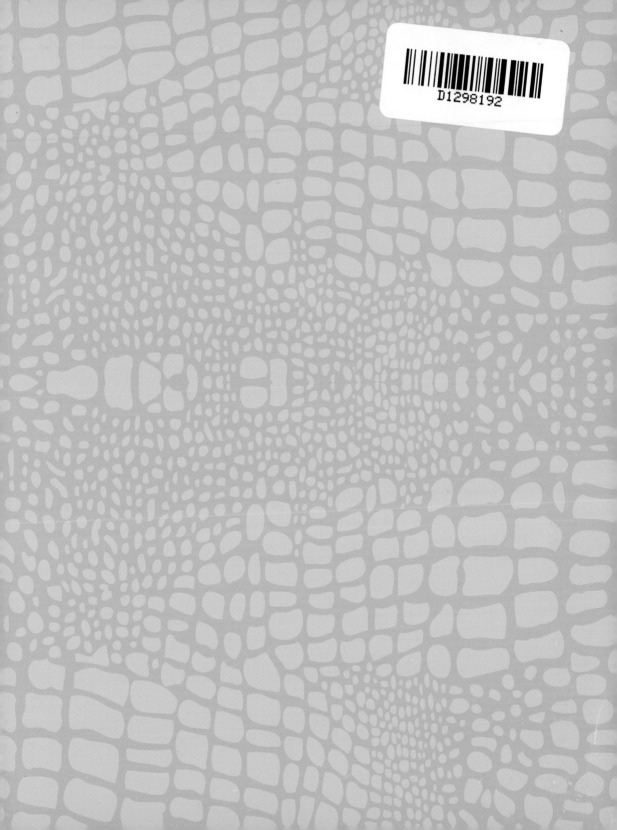

This edition published by Parragon Books Ltd in 2014
and distributed by

Parragon Inc.
440 Park Avenue South, 13th Floor
New York, NY 10016
www.parragon.com

ISBN 978-1-4723-4153-2

Printed in China

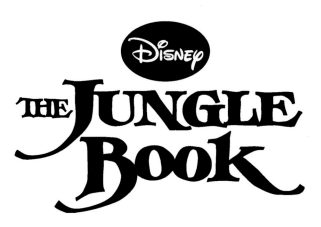

Read the story, then turn over the book
to read another story!

Bath • New York • Cologne • Melbourne • Delhi
Hong Kong • Shenzhen • Singapore • Amsterdam

Deep in the jungle, Bagheera the panther was
out hunting. Suddenly, he heard a strange crying sound
coming from the river.

He followed the sound and discovered a basket with
a tiny baby boy inside.

"Why, it's a Man-cub!" he said. "This little chap needs
food and a mother's care. Perhaps Mother Wolf will look
after him."

Mother Wolf agreed to help. They named the Man-cub
Mowgli, and he grew up safe and happy in the jungle.

But everything changed when Mowgli was 10 years old. Shere Khan, the man-eating tiger, heard about the Man-cub and came searching for him.

The wolves agreed that Bagheera should take the boy back to the Man-village where he would be safe.

So the next morning, Bagheera and Mowgli set off on their long journey. Mowgli was angry and upset. He didn't want to leave his home in the jungle.

When darkness fell, Bagheera and Mowgli climbed a
tree and settled down to sleep on a branch. Nearby, hiding
under some leaves, was Kaa the python.

As soon as Bagheera was asleep, Kaa slithered
toward the Man-cub. His shining eyes seemed to have
a magic power, and Mowgli quickly began to sink into
a deep trance.

Slowly, Kaa started to wind himself around the boy, ready to swallow him up!

Suddenly, Bagheera woke up and sprang at Kaa. He struck the snake with his claws and sent him slithering away into the jungle.

At dawn, Mowgli was woken by a very loud noise.
He looked down from the tree and saw Colonel Hathi
and the Dawn Patrol marching along.

"Hup, two, three, four! Hup, two, three, four!"
trumpeted the elephant.

Mowgli jumped down from the tree, got on all fours, and joined the end of the parade behind a baby elephant. He had lots of fun, copying everything the little elephant did!

Eventually, Bagheera caught up with Mowgli and wanted to keep going toward the Man-village.

But Mowgli refused to go. He grabbed a tree trunk and held on tightly.

Bagheera was very angry and ran off, leaving the Man-cub all alone.

It wasn't long before Mowgli met a friendly bear named Baloo. He told Baloo how much he wanted to stay in the jungle.

"No problem!" Baloo said, "I'll look after you!"

Baloo enjoyed teaching his new friend all about the 'bare necessities of life.' Soon, Mowgli could fight like a bear, growl like a bear, and even scratch like a bear!

Later that afternoon, Mowgli and Baloo waded into
the river to keep cool. Mowgli sat on Baloo's belly as they
gently floated along. It was very peaceful, and Baloo
soon fell asleep.

But watching from some trees was a group of monkeys
who were waiting to kidnap Mowgli.

The monkeys sprang out from their hiding place and grabbed the Man-cub.

Baloo woke with a jump, but it was too late! The monkeys were already carrying Mowgli off to the ruined temple where they lived.

Luckily, Bagheera heard Mowgli's cries and rushed to the river to help. He found Baloo, who explained what had happened.

"We need a rescue plan," Bagheera said.

At the ruined temple, Louie, King of the Apes, was
sitting on his throne waiting for the Man-cub to arrive.

"So, you're here at last!" Louie cried, as Mowgli was
dropped beside him.

Louie offered to help Mowgli stay in the jungle.
In return, he wanted to learn the secret of Man's red fire.

But before Mowgli could explain that he didn't know
the secret, Louie declared that they would have a great
feast in honor of their guest.

Baloo and Bagheera reached the temple just in time to see Louie leap from his throne and start to sing and dance in celebration of the Man-cub's arrival.

As Mowgli's feet began to tap to the music, he forgot his troubles and joined in the fun.

"Baloo," whispered Bagheera. "You distract the monkeys while I rescue Mowgli."

Baloo had an idea . . . He dressed in coconut shells and leaves to make himself look like a lady ape. Then he waved at Louie.

The King thought the lady ape was very beautiful, and rushed over to ask her to dance. He had no idea that it was really Baloo in disguise!

But as Baloo danced, his disguise began to fall off. The angry
monkeys realized they had been tricked and started to attack him.
Just as Bagheera rushed over to help, Baloo knocked over a pillar.

The temple came crashing down on top of the monkeys. Luckily,
Baloo and Bagheera managed to drag Mowgli to safety. The three
friends ran deep into the jungle and found a place to rest.

That night, Bagheera and Baloo kept watch over
Mowgli as he slept. It was time to discuss their young
friend's future . . .

"The Man-cub must go to the Man-village," said Bagheera, "It's not safe for him to stay in the jungle." Baloo, remembering Shere Khan, had to admit that Bagheera was right. So the next morning, Baloo led Mowgli off toward the Man-village.

When the Man-cub found out where they were headed, he was very angry.

"You don't want me to stay—you're just like Bagheera!" he shouted.

But before Baloo could explain, Mowgli ran off into the jungle.

It wasn't long before Shere Khan spotted Mowgli in the distance. Emerging from the shadows, the tiger gave a loud roar.

He leaped at Mowgli, taking the Man-cub by surprise.

But Shere Khan stopped in mid-leap and fell to the ground—Baloo had caught him by the tail!

Shere Khan roared with rage as he dragged Baloo behind
him, but the brave bear was determined not to let go.
Eventually, the furious tiger managed to flip Baloo over
his head. The bear hit the ground with a mighty crash.

Mowgli ran over to Baloo, who was lying very still on the ground. "Please get up, Baloo!" he cried.

Bagheera came over to comfort Mowgli. "Baloo was very brave," the panther said.

"Was?" gulped Mowgli. "You mean . . . Baloo's dead?"

But before Bagheera had a chance to reply, Baloo sat up and rubbed his eyes. He wasn't dead after all!

Mowgli laughed and threw his arms around the big bear's neck.

Suddenly, a lightning bolt struck a nearby tree, which burst into flames. Shere Khan was terrified! Fire was the only thing that frightened him.

Seeing his chance to get back at the tiger, Mowgli picked up a burning branch. The Man-cub tied the burning branch to the tiger's tail.

Shere Khan screamed as he clawed the branch away. Then he fled into the jungle—never to be seen again!

The three friends continued toward the Man-village. Suddenly, they heard someone singing across the river.

Mowgli peered through the trees and saw a young girl kneeling by the river.

"Isn't she pretty!" cried Mowgli, climbing a tree to have a closer look. The girl turned and smiled. Mowgli shyly smiled back. When she began to walk off toward the Man-village, Mowgli ran to join her.

Baloo and Bagheera felt very sad that their young friend was leaving. But they knew he would now be happy and safe.

The End

Now turn over the book
for another classic Disney tale!

Now turn over the book
for another classic Disney tale!

Some time later, the animals and birds made their way again to the foot of Pride Rock. Watched by the lions, Pumbaa, and Timon, Rafiki picked up a tiny cub. He showed the new prince—the son of King Simba and Queen Nala—to the cheering crowd below.

The End

Nala went to Simba's side. "Welcome home!" she whispered. As they smiled at each other, it started to rain. The heavy drops soaked the dry ground, and streambeds filled up once more. The plains came back to life, and the herds returned.

Scar lunged at Simba, determined to kill him just as he had Mufasa. In the fierce battle that followed, Simba finally heaved Scar over the cliff face. Scar called to the hyenas to save him, but Nala and the lionesses drove them back. Simba was victorious!

Back at Pride Rock, the rains had been late coming and the land was dry. The hyenas paced impatiently around King Scar. "We're starving," they howled. "The herds have gone. There's nothing left to eat." Storm clouds gathered in the sky and a lightning bolt scorched the ground. As the dry grasses caught on fire, flames swept toward Pride Rock. A lion appeared through the smoke. It was Simba!

The reflection rose into the sky, and Simba heard
Mufasa's voice:

"Simba. You must take your place in the Circle
of Life. You are my son and the one true king." Then
the reflection and Rafiki disappeared.

That night Simba lay by a stream thinking. He heard a noise
and looked up.

"Come with me," said Rafiki. "I will take you to your father."

Simba followed him in wonder to the edge of the stream.
As Simba looked into the water, his reflection gradually
changed shape and became his father's!

Simba showed Nala his favorite places in the jungle.
"It's beautiful," she said. "I can see why you like it—but
it's not your home. You're hiding from the future."
She turned and left her friend alone.

Many years later, deep in a cave, Rafiki stared at a picture of a lion. "It is time," he said, smiling, and prepared to leave.

The very next day Simba rescued Pumbaa from a hungry lioness—it was Nala! The two friends were delighted to see each other again. Nala told Simba about Scar's reign of terror at Pride Rock and begged him to return. "With you alive, Scar has no right to the throne," she said.

"I can't go back. I'm not fit to be a king," Simba said sadly.

"You could be," Nala told him.

"Thanks for your help," said Simba, "but it doesn't matter. I have nowhere to go."

"Why not stay with us?" said Timon kindly. "Put your past behind you. Remember! *Hakuna matata*—no worries! That's the way we live."

Simba thought for a moment and decided to stay in the jungle with his new friends.

Eventually Simba opened his eyes. A warthog named
Pumbaa and a meerkat named Timon were gazing down
at him. They poured water into his dry mouth.

"You nearly died," said Pumbaa. "We saved you."

As Scar returned to take the royal throne at Pride Rock for himself, Simba stumbled exhausted and frightened through the grasslands toward the jungle. He took a few more shaky steps and collapsed. Hungry vultures circled above him.

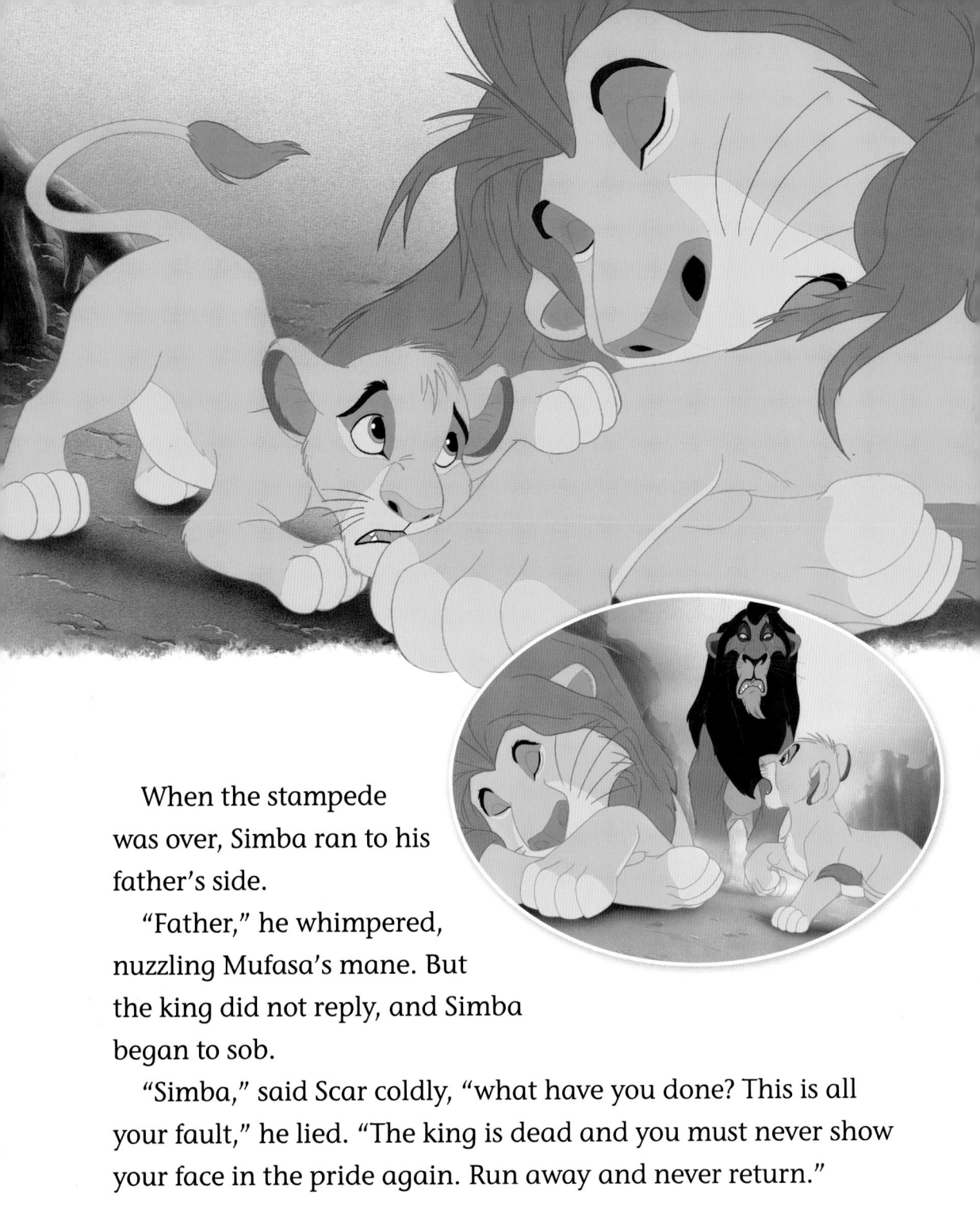

When the stampede
was over, Simba ran to his
father's side.

"Father," he whimpered,
nuzzling Mufasa's mane. But
the king did not reply, and Simba
began to sob.

"Simba," said Scar coldly, "what have you done? This is all
your fault," he lied. "The king is dead and you must never show
your face in the pride again. Run away and never return."

He fell onto an overhanging rock as the wildebeest swept by him. Looking up, he saw his brother.

"Scar, help me!" he cried. But Scar just leaned over and whispered, "Long live the king!" Then he pushed Mufasa into the path of the trampling wildebeest.

By the next day, Scar had devised another plan to get rid
of Mufasa and Simba. He led Simba to the bottom of a gorge
and told him to wait for his father. Then the hyenas started
a stampede among a herd of wildebeest.

At that moment, Mufasa was walking along a ridge with Zazu.
"Simba!" he cried. "I'm coming!"

The king raced down the gorge and rescued his son, but he
could not save himself.

The moon shone brightly above them and the stars twinkled in the dark sky.

Mufasa stopped. "Look at the stars! From there the great kings of the past look down on us. Just remember that they'll always be there to guide you, and so will I."

Simba nodded. "I'll remember."

Mufasa sent Nala and Zazu ahead and walked home with his son. "Simba, I'm disappointed in you. You disobeyed me and put yourself and others in great danger."

Simba felt terrible. "I was only trying to be brave like you," he tried to explain.

"Being brave doesn't mean you go looking for trouble," said the king gently.

Simba took a deep breath and tried to roar—but only a squeaky rumble came out. The hyenas laughed hysterically.

Simba took another deep breath.

ROAARR! The three hyenas looked around into the eyes of—King Mufasa!

The hyenas fled, howling into the mist.

"This is the elephant graveyard!" Simba cried. He was
looking at a skull when he saw Zazu, his father's adviser.

"You must leave here immediately!" Zazu commanded.
"You are in great danger."

But it was already too late! They were trapped.
Three hyenas had surrounded them, laughing menacingly.

Simba raced ahead across the plains, leading Nala to the forbidden place. Eventually they reached a pile of bones, and Simba knew they had arrived.

"It's creepy here," said Nala. "Where are we?"

Simba hurried away to find his best friend, a young lioness named Nala. Even though he knew it was wrong, Simba had decided to visit the elephant graveyard with Nala that very day.

He had no idea that Scar had ordered three hyenas to go to the elephant graveyard, too. Scar wanted them to kill the cub as the first step in his plan to take over Mufasa's kingdom.

Later that day, Simba met his uncle, Scar. The cub
proudly told him that he had seen the whole of his
future kingdom.

"Even beyond the northern border?" Scar asked slyly.

"Well, no," said Simba sadly. "My father has forbidden
me to go there."

"Quite right," said Scar. "Only the bravest lions go there.
An elephant graveyard is no place for a young prince."

Time passed quickly for little Simba. There was so much to learn. One morning, the king showed his son around the kingdom. "Remember," Mufasa warned, "a good king must respect all creatures, for we exist together in the great Circle of Life."

They watched in silence as Rafiki, a wise
old baboon, raised the lion cub high in the air.
The clouds parted and the sun's rays shone
down on the future king. Slowly Rafiki lowered
his arms and took Simba back to his proud
parents, King Mufasa and Queen Sarabi.

It was a very special day.

As the morning sun rose high over the African plain, animals and birds gathered at the foot of Pride Rock.

"There he is!" one of them cried suddenly. "There's the new prince!" Everyone cheered and stamped their feet. "Welcome, Prince Simba!" they shouted.

THE
LION KING

Read the story, then turn over the book
to read another story!

PaRragon

Bath · New York · Cologne · Melbourne · Delhi
Hong Kong · Shenzhen · Singapore · Amsterdam

This edition published by Parragon Books Ltd in 2014
and distributed by

Parragon Inc.
440 Park Avenue South, 13th Floor
New York, NY 10016
www.parragon.com

ISBN 978-1-4723-4153-2

Printed in China